Dino FC

THE GREAT KIT CATASTROPHE

KEITH BRUMPTON

First published in 2010 by Usborne Publishing Ltd., Usborne House,
83-85 Saffron Hill, London EC1N 8RT, England.
www.usborne.com

A CIP catalogue record for this book is available from the British Library.

JFMA JJASOND/15 00436/3 ISBN 9781409504856
Printed in the UK.

DINO FC

Dear Dino-soccer fan,

As you'll probably know I'm player-manager
of Dino FC. Thanks to all of you for
your texts and letters of support. Thanks
also to our mascot of last week, Oliver
Dimetrodon. I hope the goalpost falling on
you wasn't too painful. Archie certainly
has a very hard shot. Get well soon, a signed
programme is on its way.

Now we've got an important cup game
coming up and I'm looking for a win!

All the best

Terry Triceratops

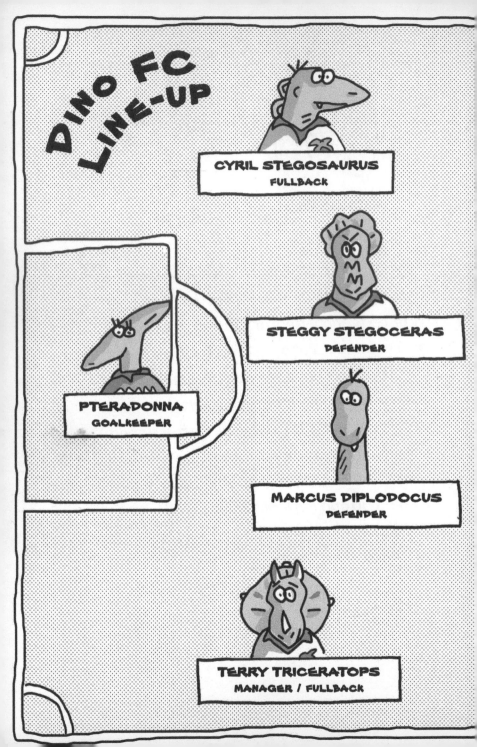

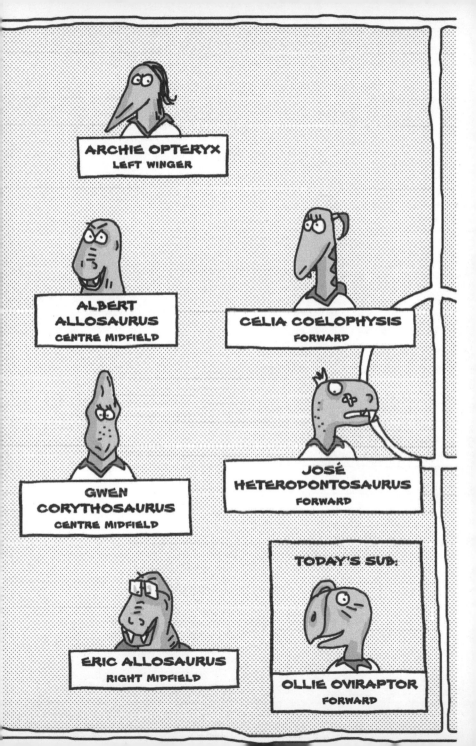

It wasn't thunder. It wasn't an earthquake.
It was the sound of Marcus Diplodocus,
Dino FC's giant centre half, sprinting up
and down on the spot.

A cloudy morning had just dawned on the team's training ground, and player-manager Terry Triceratops was busy putting his side through their paces before an important couple of matches.

While most of the players were exercising quite happily, at the back of the field, two members of the team were grumbling to one another as they skipped: Steggy Stegoceras, Dino FC's hard-headed defender, and fashion-conscious forward, Celia Coelophysis.

"I can't believe we have to train in the same kit we wear to play our matches in," moaned Steggy, while watching that no heavy-footed dinosaur in front of him accidentally jumped on his toes as he skipped. "In fact, isn't it time we had some new kit altogether?"

9

"Who's worn and out of date?" wheezed Ollie Oviraptor as he exercised nearby. Ollie was the team's oldest player and he always worried people were talking about his age.

DON'T WORRY, WE'RE NOT TALKING ABOUT YOU.

"We're just saying that it's time we had some new kit."

"Ah yes, I agree," replied Ollie. "The elastic has completely gone in my shorts.

I'm frightened I'll lose them when I run."

"Lucky you don't do much running then," joked Steggy, but fortunately Ollie didn't hear him.

"What's all this chatter?" asked Terry, spotting the grumbling dinosaurs at the far end of the training pitch.

"Heart-rates," interjected Cyril Stegosaurus, Terry's loyal vice captain and fullback.

Terry nodded, then turned to Steggy and Celia. "What's wrong, guys?"

"We want some new kit," snapped Steggy, who always said exactly what he was thinking.

YOU HAVE TO ADMIT IT, BOSS...THE OLD ONE LOOKS A BIT, ER...

...RUBBISH!

Terry was surprised to hear the team complaining about their kit, but, thinking about it, he had to admit the old strips were looking very worn.

The yellow and blue colour on their shirts had faded, and the tree-motif badges were frayed.

While other teams had both home and away strips, Dino FC didn't even have any training bibs left – they'd all been ripped to shreds during a "friendly" practice match against a team of velociraptors.

Terry realized it would be great for the team to get new kit, but how could hard-up Dino FC ever afford it?

Terry knew exactly what state the club's finances were in. A terrible state. The club bank balance read zero and even the box of loose change that Terry kept tucked away for a "rainy day" was almost empty. Even if there had been any cash available, Terry would much rather have used it to buy a new striker or extra balls for training (Marcus Diplodocus regularly lost a few balls each week when his headers landed in the nearby volcano).

ER, IF I COULD JUST HAVE A WORD, EVERYBODY? ABOUT THE KIT SITUATION...

There were nods all round.

"…But we just don't have the cash. Plus, it's not about the shirt – or what kit we wear – it's about playing for each other and for the club!"

"Exactly," nodded Cyril Stegosaurus, who could always be relied on to back his manager one hundred per cent.

He flapped his arms to demonstrate.

Cyril's shirt ripped down one side and flapped in the breeze like an old towel on a washing line.

"Er, don't worry, boss, I'll get it sewn up this evening," Cyril mumbled, trying to pull the edges of his torn shirt together to cover the gaping holes.

"Okay, everyone, back to training!" shouted Terry, clapping his hands.

TWICE ROUND THE PITCH AND TWENTY PRESS-UPS FOR THE LAST ONE TO FINISH!

The squad set off at a brisk run, except for Marcus Diplodocus. He couldn't run fast even if he wanted to, but because his stride was so long, he managed to avoid last place. That went to poor Cyril.

"Sorry I was last, skipper," Cyril puffed, as he completed the last of his twenty press-ups. "The tears in my shirt were flapping in front of my eyes so I couldn't see where I was going."

And so another Dino FC training session came to an end, and the team guessed they would be wearing the same old kit for the rest of the season. But none of them imagined that the very next day something would happen to change Terry's mind...

It was early morning and Terry was at home brushing his teeth when he heard a loud knock at his tree. It was the club chairman, Danny Deinonychus.

Relationships between Terry and his chairman were about as warm as a block of ice. Every time they met Terry worried in case he was going to be sacked. And now there stood his chairman, looking very serious in his smart business clothes, and removing a piece of meat from between his front teeth.

"Good morning." mumbled Terry, nervously.

"Team kit," replied Danny in a snarl, totally ignoring Terry's greeting. "I was watching you lot train the other day and it looks very shabby. Bad for my image. The club needs a new look."

"Er, I'm not sure about that," began Terry, still convinced they couldn't afford to spend money on new shirts and shorts.

Danny shoved a piece of paper into Terry's hoof.

Terry's expression brightened. "Wow, that's great!" he beamed. "The team will be over the moon."

"So they should be," snapped Danny. "I want you all to come up with ideas for the new look."

Terry smiled as he read the note he was holding.

COMPETITION!!!!!!!

OPEN TO: ALL DINO FC PLAYERS

THE CHALLENGE: TO DESIGN THE

NEW KIT FOR DINO FC

FIRST PRIZE — COMPLIMENTARY PASS FOR THE DANNY DEINONYCHUS SWAMPY HEALTH SPA *

* Conditions apply

* (winner must be over 10, n health problems, and .. for treatment)

Terry suddenly felt much more cheerful. If someone else was paying for the kit then it would be fantastic to have new shirts and shorts. It might even give the team a morale boost before their next match.

"Thanks, Mr. Deinonychus," he beamed, but his chairman had already left, taking an important business call on his shell-phone as he vanished down the road.

SORRY, CLIFF, RECEPTION'S REALLY BAD...

A contest to design a new look for Dino FC! Terry felt sure his squad would have lots of amazing ideas...and he'd already got a few himself!

CHAPTER 4

Terry let the team complete their five-a-side practice match before telling them the news about the design-a-new-strip competition.

"I thought you said we couldn't afford new kit," grumbled Steggy, who was never happy.

The squad chattered excitedly amongst themselves. It seemed everyone had an idea about how the new kit should look.

"I'm thinking hot pink," said Celia, her imagination already racing to the photo shoot *Hello Dino!* magazine would ask her to do.

"I'd prefer something traditional," offered Ollie Oviraptor.

WITH LONG SHORTS TO HIDE MY WRINKLY KNEES.

Terry told the team they had until tomorrow's training session to get their ideas together. Only the team's vice captain, Cyril Stegosaurus, didn't seem happy. "We'd be better off worrying about Saturday's game than what colour shirts to wear," he muttered, while munching on some ferns.

"I know what you mean, Cyril, but this contest is just a bit of fun, and who knows, it might help build team spirit. Then tomorrow we can get straight back to business," said Terry.

Cyril shrugged his shoulders and hoped his boss was right.

For the rest of the day, the area around the training ground was alive with the sounds of scratching heads and squeaky pens as the dinosaurs set about drawing and colouring in their designs.

Every member of the Dino FC team wanted to have a go at designing a new kit and a chance to win the first prize.

Gwen Corythosaurus scribbled cheerfully. Twins, Eric and Albert Allosaurus, argued over whose crayon was whose.

Marcus Diplodocus gave himself a stiff neck bending down to look at his drawing. Celia Coelophysis imagined herself already at the Swampy Health Spa, enjoying a beauty treatment.

NOT THAT I NEED IT OF COURSE.

Even Terry had been thinking long and hard about what strip he'd like to wear. Being a total football professional he'd done some research on which colours made dinosaurs look fiercest. Red and yellow were supposed to be the best at getting this effect, so Terry put them into his design, thinking it

might help to scare the opposition.

"Anything to give us the edge," he thought, as he coloured in his design. "I wonder what the rest of the guys have come up with?"

The next day, it was just as Cyril Stegosaurus had feared – the competition proved to be a big distraction. The whole team turned up to training looking exhausted because they had stayed up all night finishing their designs.

Gwen Corythosaurus, the team's midfielder, couldn't stop yawning; Marcus Diplodocus kept dozing off, and Ollie Oviraptor had big bags under his eyes (but then again he always did).

Terry started the squad out with a simple routine, dribbling the ball between a line of fossils, but no one could concentrate.

Normally Pteradonna, the team's flying goalkeeper, was a very quiet and sensible member of the squad. If she couldn't concentrate on training, then Terry knew that no one could. Maybe he should just get this silly competition out of the way?

"Okay, everybody," he sighed, "hand in your entries."

He was almost flattened in the rush.

OOF!

"If they moved like that during matches we'd be top of the league," Terry muttered to himself, half buried under a forest of dinosaur legs.

"Who gets to judge the winning entry?" asked Steggy, suspiciously.

Terry hadn't even thought of that.

"Er, I don't know," he answered.
"Maybe the chairman."

"We could ask the fans to vote,"
suggested Archie Opteryx, the team's speedy
winger.

But Dino FC didn't have many fans, so
after the training session, Terry asked the
team's "fan of the year" and only season
ticket holder, Martin Millipede, to choose the
best design.

Martin took a long time thinking about it, because millipedes only have small brains.

"I like this one best," he said, after about an hour.

Terry looked at the entry Martin had chosen and had to admit it looked great.

He handed Martin a signed photo of the team.

"Did I win? Did I win?" asked Celia, jumping up and down on the spot.

"Are we playing in orange?" asked Gwen, who had featured orange triangles in her crazy-looking design.

Terry answered all their questions by holding up the winning entry. "There's no name on it," he said.

"Er, it's mine I think," came a voice from the back. All heads turned to a rather embarrassed-looking Cyril Stegosaurus.

"Hang on," said Steggy, feeling cross that his own design hadn't won.

Terry suddenly realized why the colours had looked familiar.

"Well I like our kit the way it is," answered Cyril, truthfully. "It's traditional."

As grumbling broke out all around the training ground, Terry raised his hoof for calm.

"Look, Cyril has come up with a great design, and won the competition fair and square. It might be the same old colours but at least we'll have new shirts and shorts that fit us properly."

The grumbling died down and even Steggy had to admit that Terry had a point.

That evening, as the sun set and herds of dinosaurs trundled home in the rush hour, Terry dropped off the winning design at Danny's luxury treetop mansion, and was told that the new kit would be ready in time for their next match.

"You lot will look like a proper team for once," he growled at Terry.

As Terry walked home he knew he was under a lot of pressure. He really hoped the new kit would help Dino FC raise their game.

Match day dawned bright and sunny, with just a cloud or two drifting high over the nearby volcanoes.

Terry was woken early by a delivery dinosaur. He was carrying a large box with the word "Dannykit" printed on the side.

Even though Terry hadn't been that
bothered about getting a new kit at first,
now he couldn't wait to see what it would
look like.

"Sorry. I've been told to collect
payment," replied the delivery dinosaur,
tapping his tail impatiently. "I'll have to
take the box away again if you can't pay."

Terry had no choice but to use the "rainy day" fund hidden beneath the roots of his tree house.

He met Cyril on his way into the ground, and told him what had happened.

"That's typical of that crooked chairman," Cyril glowered angrily.

"I'm sure it's just a mistake," answered Terry, secretly thinking Cyril might be right. "I'll speak to Danny after the game. That thirty bushels is thirty bushels we can't afford!"

That day's match was against a powerful side, called Supersaurus Celtic. They were lying second in the Dinosaur Premier League and Dino FC would have to play well to beat them.

"Me first! Me first!" shouted Celia as Terry unpacked the new kit: pale yellow shirts, with blue trim and a large palm tree logo in the middle of the shirt. Exactly the same as they had always worn, but with no rips, stains or tears.

"We're going to play *so* well today,"
smiled Archie Opteryx. "Supersaurus won't
know what's hit them!" But as he pulled on
his dazzling new shirt he was surprised to
find it almost reached his knees.

ER, IS THERE A
SMALLER SHIRT
ANYWHERE?

There wasn't. All the shirts were the
same size! And so were the shorts!

The team had hoped to look cool as they ran out to start the match in their new kit, but instead they looked completely ridiculous.

Marcus Diplodocus looked like he was wearing cycling shorts. Pteradonna's goalkeeping top was so big it swamped her. Steggy's shirt was so tight he couldn't bend down to tie up his laces.

Dino FC kicked off feeling so preoccupied about their kit, it was no surprise when Supersaurus took the lead with their first attack. A long kick from their goalie wasn't cleared by Marcus, who could hardly move in his tight shorts.

Pteradonna fumbled for the ball from inside her giant shirt, but it bounced off a post and into the back of the net.

"Booooo!" jeered the crowd (including chairman Danny Deinonychus, who'd just arrived).

Led by a determined Terry, Dino FC tried to fight back, but their new kit wasn't helping. As Terry tried to pass the ball back to Pteradonna, his shiny new shirt dazzled the young goalie's eyes and she missed the ball completely.

It was an own goal. And two-nil to Supersaurus! Dino FC were rocked back on their heels.

Up in the DBC (Dinosaur Broadcasting Corporation) commentary box, expert commentators, Mark Megalosaurus and Gary Seymouria, didn't fancy the chances of Terry's team ever getting back into the match.

Half-time came and Rumbley Stadium
resounded to loud jeers.

Terry's half-time talk was short and to
the point: "There's no time to do anything
about the kit. Forget about the problems
and remember the fans."

The second half kicked off with Dino FC battling hard to get back into the game. Archie streaked down the wing, beat two lumbering defenders, and whipped in a cross. José Heterodontosaurus threw himself at the ball and it rocketed into the back of the net.

One-two. Game on! But try as they might, Dino FC couldn't get an equalizer.

THE MORE THEY RAN, THE HOTTER THEY GOT.

AND THE HOTTER THEY GOT, THE MORE THEY SWEATED.

The new shirts were made from some strange cheap material that didn't let the air in or out, and soon the shirts were so heavy with sweat, the team could hardly run at all.

Even Eric and Albert, who were pretty fit, were so tired they couldn't be bothered to argue.

Supersaurus Celtic scored three more goals
before the ref blew his nose to end the match.

Boos and jeers rang out again as the defeated Dino FC players trudged off the pitch, leaving a trail of sweat behind them. The match had been a disaster!

"That's it!" snapped Terry, as the team sat stunned in their dressing cave. "I'm going to take this kit back to the chairman right now."

Even Celia and Steggy, who'd wanted the new strip the most, admitted that they would have played better in the old kit.

Marcus Diplodocus's shirt was now so tight and soggy it took three of the team to pull it off him...

Terry jammed the sweaty new kit back into the box it had arrived in, and then Cyril helped him carry it all the way to Chairman Danny's very posh tree house.

Terry knocked and waited. And waited. He was nervous and didn't know exactly how he would explain to Danny that the new kit was rubbish.

When Danny did appear he looked so fierce that Terry could hardly speak.

"Dreadful performance today, Triceratops. Why was the between-the-sticks player so bad?" he began. (He meant the goalkeeper – Danny didn't know anything about football.)

"Pteradonna, you mean?" asked Terry.

YES, SHE DIDN'T CATCH A THING ALL DAY. AND THE REST OF YOU WERE JUST AS BAD. I COULD HAVE DONE BETTER MYSELF.

"It was the kit," interrupted Terry. "It's no good. We can't play in it. And I had to pay for it out of my rainy day fund."

"Er, change it?" stammered Terry hopefully.

"No chance, Triceratops. If you don't like the lovely new kit I had made for you, well, tough!"

Before Terry or Cyril could argue, another call came in on Danny's shell-phone and he turned and climbed back up into his tree house.

"That didn't go well did it, boss?" sighed a gloomy-looking Cyril.

"It sure didn't," replied Terry. "I've spent our rainy day fund, we've got a set of kit we can't wear and I've thrown out the old kit. The DFA cup quarter-final is in two days' time. It's a huge match for us. What on earth are we going to do?"

CHAPTER 9

As Terry lay in bed that night he remembered his good friend Cyril's parting words: "What you always say, boss, is keep a cool head." He was right. Terry knew he had to calm down and tackle one problem at a time, if he was ever to sort out this mess.

The first step was to get rid of the useless new kit. Terry didn't want to throw it all away though, because that would be a waste. He thought he knew some dinosaurs that'd be grateful for new shirts and shorts — a bunch of young dinosaurs who often kicked a ball around by the old Permian Forest.

Terry headed there early the next morning.

When he explained to the youngsters that they could have new shirts and shorts for free, they were thrilled, even though it meant wearing Dino FC colours when almost all of them supported wealthier, more successful clubs.

"Thanks, Mr. Triceratops," beamed a young brachiosaurus, who recognized the Dino FC manager from the back pages of the local paper. Terry told them about the big DFA match coming up and they wished him luck.

Result! Next, Terry had to recover the old kit, which he'd put out with the rubbish. He hoped that it hadn't been taken away yet. Luckily, the ripped and faded shirts and shorts were exactly where he'd left them, beneath a tall ginkgo tree.

They didn't smell too good, but a quick wash in the stream would sort that out.

Now all Terry had to do was to get the team focused on their next match – the DFA Cup quarter-final tie against the high-flying Pterodactyl Flappers...

Back in their old kit, the team trained hard
for the game and quickly got over the
disappointment of the great kit catastrophe
(except for Steggy, who kept grumbling right
up to kick-off time).

Terry gave one of his most inspiring team talks ever and warned his players to be careful at corners and during set pieces because the Pterodactyl Flappers were excellent in the air.

The team linked arms in a circle and concentrated hard for a few moments, then shouted the team name and ran out onto the pitch, nervous but at least feeling comfortable in their familiar old shirts and shorts.

After their last defeat the home crowd in the volcano end was very small and quiet.

As the game kicked off, the whole team tried hard to remember Terry's instructions (even Archie and Marcus, who had very bad memories). They kept the ball on the ground, they tried not to give away any free kicks or corners, and when they did, they made sure they marked the other team tightly.

Pitchside interview

Dino FC made only one mistake. There was a corner from the left, Eric Allosaurus slipped and the Pterodactyl he was marking rose unchallenged to nod the ball into the net. One-nil to the Flappers.

While Eric argued with his brother about the mistake, Terry shouted that they could still win the game. But the team looked downhearted. It had been a tough week.

Just when all seemed lost, Terry heard a strange sound coming from the volcano end. Cheering! It was coming from the Dino FC fans, but there seemed to be a lot more of them now, and they were making an awful lot of noise.

Looking over in their direction, Terry saw, to his surprise, a familiar group of young dinosaurs, all wearing the team's colours and chanting:

It was the young kids he'd given the kit to. They'd decided to come and support their local team and now their cheers made it sound like the ground was full.

The rest of the team heard the kids too. They seemed to grow a metre taller (which is useful if you're playing against pterodactyls).

With Terry leading the way like a dinosaur possessed, Dino FC upped their game and within five minutes they were level – Albert Allosaurus blasting the ball home from ten metres out!

With five minutes to go, and the game tied at one-all, the crowd urged Dino FC forward. Shot after shot rained in on the Flappers' goal as Terry's team began to dominate the game.

But the winning goal wouldn't come.

Then, finally, a brilliant dribble by Celia ended when she was flattened by an outstretched wing inside the penalty area.

And a penalty it was.

Terry usually took the spot kicks himself, but his legs felt weak and he wondered for a moment if he should ask someone else to take this one. But then he looked up at the terraces, saw the excited home fans, and knew this was down to him.

He wiped his sweaty hoofs on his
familiar old shirt, took three steps back, ran
in, and stroked the ball to the left-hand side
of the goal.

He hadn't kicked the ball hard but the Flappers' goalkeeper had dived to his right. Too soon as it turned out. The ball nestled sweetly in the back of the net.

Goal!

It was chaos!

The crowd erupted. And so did a nearby volcano.

Dino FC had won two-one. They were
through to the semi-finals of the cup.

Led by Terry, the Dino FC players ran across to their fans and gave them a special thank-you wave. They might even have thrown

them their shirts, but they only had one set
and didn't want to lose them!

Chairman Danny joined the team on the pitch and waved to the fans as if he had won the game himself. Terry didn't mind. He knew that if the team kept playing at that standard then they really could go all the way and win their first-ever trophy.

The team went off to shower.

"I always said these old shirts were lucky," said Steggy (who'd never said any such thing).

"It's not about the shirt," Terry said.

Everyone cheered.

"This water's cold," grumbled Steggy.

"When can we get a new shower?"

Terry rolled his eyes and smiled.

THE END

MEET THE PLAYERS IN DINO FC

- THE CRAZIEST TEAM IN THE JURASSIC WORLD!

RUMBLEY STADIUM - THE DINO FC GROUND

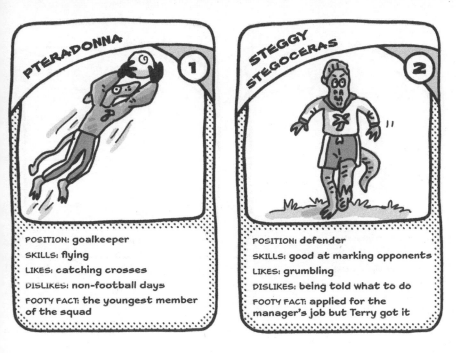

PTERADONNA

1

POSITION: goalkeeper
SKILLS: flying
LIKES: catching crosses
DISLIKES: non-football days
FOOTY FACT: the youngest member of the squad

STEGGY STEGOCERAS

2

POSITION: defender
SKILLS: good at marking opponents
LIKES: grumbling
DISLIKES: being told what to do
FOOTY FACT: applied for the manager's job but Terry got it

MARCUS DIPLODOCUS

3

POSITION: defender
SKILLS: great in the air
LIKES: heading the ball
DISLIKES: quick forwards
FOOTY FACT: last season won 76% of all headers

TERRY TRICERATOPS

4

POSITION: manager and fullback
SKILLS: tactician
LIKES: tough talking
DISLIKES: defensive football
FOOTY FACT: only player-manager in the DPL

CYRIL STEGOSAURUS

5

POSITION: **fullback**

SKILLS: **following instructions**

LIKES: **moving slowly**

DISLIKES: **anyone criticizing Terry, "the boss"**

FOOTY FACT: **the vice-captain**

ALBERT ALLOSAURUS

6

POSITION: **midfield**

SKILLS: **dealing with tricky forwards**

LIKES: **arguing with his twin**

DISLIKES: **Eric. Refs**

FOOTY FACT: **once got 21 red cards in a season**

GWEN CORYTHOSAURUS

7

POSITION: **midfield**

SKILLS: **controlling midfield**

LIKES: **playing in the rain**

DISLIKES: **hot temperatures**

FOOTY FACT: **the team's free kick specialist**

ARCHIE OPTERYX

8

POSITION: **winger**

SKILLS: **great dribbler**

LIKES: **doing ball tricks**

DISLIKES: **bumpy pitches**

FOOTY FACT: **takes the team's corners**

ERIC ALLOSAURUS

9

POSITION: **midfield**
SKILLS: **tackling, marking**
LIKES: **arguing with his twin**
DISLIKES: **Albert. Refs**
FOOTY FACT: **once got 20 red cards in a season**

CELIA COELOPHYSIS

10

POSITION: **forward**
SKILLS: **fast and graceful**
LIKES: **looking good on the pitch**
DISLIKES: **tackling or being tackled**
FOOTY FACT: **fastest player on the team**

JOSÉ HETERODONTOSAURUS

11

POSITION: **forward**
SKILLS: **falling over in the box**
LIKES: **winning penalties**
DISLIKES: **most things**
FOOTY FACT: **on average only fit for 2.3 games per season**

OLLIE OVIRAPTOR

12

POSITION: **utility player**
SKILLS: **football brain, experience**
LIKES: **resting after the match**
DISLIKES: **playing 90 minutes**
FOOTY FACT: **has been a pro for 22 seasons**

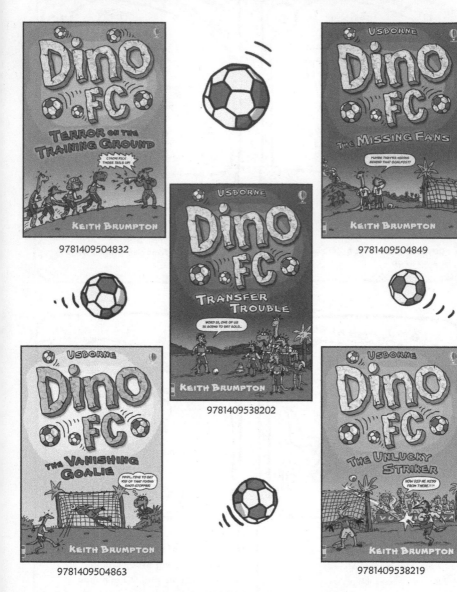